A LITTLE HOUSE CHRISTMAS

VOLUME II

Holiday Stories from the Little House Books

BY

LAURA INGALLS WILDER

ILLUSTRATED BY

GARTH WILLIAMS

HarperCollins*Publishers*

Garth Williams' artwork was colorized, with his permission, by Stephen Marchesi and Holly Jones.

HarperCollins®, ☙®, and Little House®
are trademarks of HarperCollins Publishers Inc.

A Little House Christmas Volume II:
Holiday Stories from the Little House Books

A Little House Christmas Volume II is adapted from the following books:
These Happy Golden Years, text copyright 1943, copyright renewed 1971, Roger Lea MacBride;
illustrations copyright 1953 by Garth Williams, renewed 1981 by Garth Williams;
By the Shores of Silver Lake, text copyright 1939, copyright renewed 1967, Roger Lea MacBride;
illustrations copyright 1953 by Garth Williams, renewed 1981 by Garth Williams;
The Long Winter, text copyright 1940, copyright renewed 1968, Roger Lea MacBride; illustrations
copyright 1953 by Garth Williams, renewed 1981 by Garth Williams;
Farmer Boy, text copyright 1933, copyright renewed 1961, Roger Lea MacBride; illustrations
copyright 1953 by Garth Williams, renewed 1981 by Garth Williams.

Library of Congress Cataloging-in-Publication Data
Wilder, Laura Ingalls, 1867–1957.
   A Little house Christmas, volume II: holiday stories from the Little house books / by Laura
Ingalls Wilder ; illustrated by Garth Williams.
      p.   cm.
   Summary: A collection of stories describing the various Christmas celebrations of a pioneer girl
and her family.
   ISBN 0-06-027489-1.
   [1. Children's stories, American.   2. Christmas—Fiction.   3. Frontier and pioneer life—Fiction.
4. Family life—Fiction.]   I. Williams, Garth, ill. II. Title.
PZ7.W6461Lg   1997   93-24537
[Fic]—dc20   CIP
                                                                                              AC

1   2   3   4   5   6   7   8   9   10
❖
First Edition

CONTENTS

ONCE UPON A TIME, *a little girl named Laura Ingalls lived in a little log cabin in the Big Woods of Wisconsin with her Pa, her Ma, her big sister Mary, and her baby sister Carrie. Laura had many adventures as she traveled west across the prairie with her family in their covered wagon, and when Laura was grown, she told of these adventures in the Little House books. Some of the most wonderful stories in these books tell of the merry Christmas celebrations Laura and her family shared together on the shores of Silver Lake and in the town of De Smet, where Laura and Almanzo fell in love. Here is the second volume of Christmas stories from the pioneer days of long ago, gathered together in a very special holiday storybook. Merry Christmas to all!*

CHRISTMAS FOR FARMER BOY

It's Christmastime on the Wilder farm in Malone, New York. While Laura is growing up in a little log house on the western prairie, Almanzo is a little farmer boy learning to help his parents and brother and sisters mind the farm. This year the aunts and uncles and all the cousins are coming to spend Christmas together on the farm. Almanzo knows that if he is a good boy, he may find a treat in his stocking on Christmas morning. And he can't wait for Christmas Day, when he is sure to have the most delicious dinner of the whole year.

Christmas

For a long time it seemed that Christmas would never come. On Christmas, Uncle Andrew and Aunt Delia, Uncle Wesley and Aunt Lindy, and all the cousins were coming to dinner. It would be the best dinner of the whole year. And a good boy might get something in his stocking. Bad boys found nothing but switches in their stockings on Christmas morning. Almanzo tried to be good for so long that he could hardly stand the strain.

But at last it was the day before Christmas and Alice and Royal and Eliza Jane were home again. The girls were cleaning the whole house, and Mother was baking. Royal helped Father with the threshing, but Almanzo

had to help in the house. He remembered the switch, and tried to be willing and cheerful.

He had to scour the steel knives and forks, and polish the silver. He had to wear an apron around his neck. He took the scouring-brick and scraped a pile of red dust off it, and then with a wet cloth he rubbed the dust up and down on the knives and forks.

The kitchen was full of delicious smells. Newly baked bread was cooling, frosted cakes and cookies and mince pies and pumpkin pies filled the pantry shelves, cranberries bubbled on the stove. Mother was making dressing for the goose.

Outdoors, the sun was shining on the snow. The icicles twinkled all along the eaves. Far away sleigh-bells faintly jingled, and from the barns came the joyful thud-thud! thud-thud! of the flails. But when all the steel knives and forks were done, Almanzo soberly polished the silver.

Then he had to run to the attic for sage; he had to run down cellar for apples, and upstairs again for onions. He filled the woodbox. He hurried in the cold to fetch water from the pump. He thought maybe he was through, then, anyway for a minute. But no; he had to polish the dining-room side of the stove.

"Do the parlor side yourself, Eliza Jane," Mother said. "Almanzo might spill the blacking."

Almanzo's insides quaked. He knew what would happen if Mother knew about that black splotch, hidden on the parlor wall. He didn't want to get a switch in his Christmas stocking, but he would far rather find a switch there than have Father take him to the woodshed.

That night everyone was tired, and the house was so clean and neat that nobody dared touch anything. After supper Mother put the stuffed, fat goose and the little pig into the heater's oven to roast slowly all night. Father set the dampers and wound the clock. Almanzo and Royal hung clean socks on the back of a chair, and Alice and Eliza Jane hung stockings on the back of another chair.

Then they all took candles and went to bed.

It was still dark when Almanzo woke up. He felt excited, and then he remembered that this was Christmas morning. He jerked back the covers and jumped onto something alive that squirmed. It was Royal. He had forgotten that Royal was there, but he scrambled over him, yelling:

"Christmas! Christmas! Merry Christmas!"

He pulled his trousers over his nightshirt. Royal jumped out of

bed and lighted the candle. Almanzo grabbed the candle, and Royal shouted:

"Hi! Leave that be! Where's my pants?"

But Almanzo was already running downstairs. Alice and Eliza Jane were flying from their room, but Almanzo beat them. He saw his sock hanging all lumpy; he set down the candle and grabbed his sock. The first thing he pulled out was a cap, a boughten cap!

The plaid cloth was machine-woven. So was the lining. Even the sewing was machine-sewing. And the ear-muffs were buttoned over the top.

Almanzo yelled. He had not even hoped for such a cap. He looked at it, inside and out; he felt the cloth and the sleek lining. He put the cap on his head. It was a little large, because he was growing. So he could wear it a long time.

Eliza Jane and Alice were digging into their stockings and squealing, and Royal had a silk muffler. Almanzo thrust his hand into his sock again, and pulled out a nickel's worth of horehound candy. He bit off the end of one stick. The outside melted like maple sugar, but the inside was hard and could be sucked for hours.

Then he pulled out a new pair of mittens. Mother had knit the wrists and backs in a fancy stitch. He pulled out an orange, and he pulled out a little package of dried figs. And he thought that was all. He thought no boy ever had a better Christmas.

But in the toe of the sock there was still something more. It was small and thin and hard. Almanzo couldn't imagine what it was. He pulled it out, and it was a jack-knife. It had four blades.

Almanzo yelled and yelled. He snapped all the blades open, sharp and shining, and he yelled,

"Alice, look! Look, Royal! Lookee, lookee my jack-knife! Lookee my cap!"

Father's voice came out of the dark bedroom and said:

"Look at the clock."

They all looked at one another. Then Royal held up the candle and they looked at the tall clock. Its hands pointed to half past three.

Even Eliza Jane did not know what to do. They had waked up Father and Mother, an hour and a half before time to get up.

"What time is it?" Father asked.

Almanzo looked at Royal. Royal and Almanzo looked at Eliza Jane. Eliza Jane swallowed, and opened her mouth, but Alice said:

"Merry Christmas, Father! Merry Christmas, Mother! It's—it's—thirty minutes to four, Father."

The clock said, "Tick! Tock! Tick! Tock! Tick!" Then Father chuckled.

Royal opened the dampers of the heater, and Eliza Jane stirred up the kitchen fire and put the kettle on. The house was warm and cosy when Father and Mother got up, and they had a whole hour to spare. There was time to enjoy the presents.

Alice had a gold locket, and Eliza Jane had a pair of garnet earrings. Mother had knitted new lace collars and black lace mitts for them both. Royal had the silk muffler and a fine leather wallet. But Almanzo thought he had the best presents of all. It was a wonderful Christmas.

Then Mother began to hurry, and to hurry everyone else. There were the chores to do, the milk to skim, the new milk to strain and put away, breakfast to eat, vegetables to be peeled, and the whole house must be put in order and everybody dressed up before the company came.

The sun rushed up the sky. Mother was everywhere, talking all the time. "Almanzo, wash your ears! Goodness mercy, Royal, don't stand around underfoot! Eliza Jane, remember you're paring those potatoes, not slicing them, and don't leave so many eyes they can see to jump out of the pot. Count the silver, Alice, and piece it out with the steel knives and forks. The best bleached tablecloths are on the bottom shelf. Mercy on us, look at that clock!"

Sleigh-bells came jingling up the road, and Mother slammed the oven door and ran to change her apron and pin on her brooch; Alice ran downstairs and Eliza Jane ran upstairs, both of them told Almanzo to straighten his collar. Father was calling Mother to fold his cravat. Then Uncle Wesley's sleigh stopped with a last clash of bells.

Almanzo ran out, whooping, and Father and Mother came behind him, as calm as if they had never hurried in their lives. Frank and Fred and Abner and Mary tumbled out of the sleigh, all bundled up, and before Aunt Lindy had handed Mother the baby, Uncle Andrew's sleigh was coming. The yard was full of boys and the house filled with hoopskirts. The uncles stamped snow off their boots and unwound their mufflers.

Royal and Cousin James drove the sleighs into the Buggy-House; they unhitched the horses and put them in stalls and rubbed down their snowy legs.

Almanzo was wearing his boughten cap, and he showed the cousins his jack-knife. Frank's cap was old now. He had a jack-knife, but it had only three blades.

Then Almanzo showed his cousins Star and Bright, and the little bob-sled, and he let them scratch Lucy's fat white back with corncobs. He said they could look at Starlight if they'd be quiet and not scare him.

The beautiful colt twitched his tail, and came daintily stepping toward them. Then he tossed his head and shied away from Frank's hand thrust through the bars.

"You leave him be!" Almanzo said.

"I bet you don't dast go in there and get on his back," said Frank.

"I dast, but I got better sense," Almanzo told him. "I know better than to spoil that fine colt."

"How'd it spoil him?" Frank said. "Yah, you're scared he'd hurt you! You're scared of that little bitty colt!"

"I am not scared," said Almanzo. "But Father won't let me."

"I guess I'd do it if I wanted to, if I was you. I guess your father wouldn't know," Frank said.

Almanzo didn't answer, and Frank got up on the bars of the stall.

"You get down off there!" Almanzo said, and he took hold of Frank's leg. "Don't you scare that colt!"

"I'll scare him if I want to," Frank said, kicking. Almanzo hung on. Starlight was running around and around the stall, and Almanzo wanted to yell for Royal. But he knew that would frighten Starlight even more.

He set his teeth and gave a mighty tug, and Frank came tumbling down. All the horses jumped, and Starlight reared and smashed against the manger.

"I'll lick you for that," Frank said, scrambling up.

"You just try and lick me!" said Almanzo.

Royal came hurrying from the South Barn. He took Almanzo and Frank by the shoulders and marched them outdoors. Fred and Abner and John came silently after them, and Almanzo's knees wabbled. He was afraid Royal would tell Father.

"Let me catch you boys fooling around those colts again," Royal said, "and I'll tell Father and Uncle Wesley. You'll get the hides thrashed off you."

Royal shook Almanzo so hard that he couldn't tell how hard Royal was shaking Frank. Then he knocked their heads together. Almanzo saw stars.

"Let that teach you to fight. On Christmas Day! For shame!" Royal said.

"I only didn't want him to scare Starlight," Almanzo said.

"Shut up!" said Royal. "Don't be a tattle-tale. Now you behave yourselves or you'll wish you had. Go wash your hands; it's dinner-time."

They all went into the kitchen and washed their hands. Mother and the aunts and the girl cousins were taking up the Christmas dinner. The dining-table had been turned around and pulled out till it was almost as long as the dining-room, and every inch of it was loaded with good things to eat.

Almanzo bowed his head and shut his eyes tight while Father said the blessing. It was a long blessing, because this was Christmas Day. But at last Almanzo could open his eyes. He sat and silently looked at that table.

He looked at the crisp, crackling little pig lying on the blue platter with an apple in its mouth. He looked at the fat roast goose, the drumsticks sticking up, and the edges of dressing curling out. The sound of Father's knife sharpening on the whetstone made him even hungrier.

He looked at the big bowl of cranberry jelly, and at the fluffy mountain of mashed potatoes with melting butter trickling down it. He looked at the heap of mashed turnips, and the golden baked squash, and the pale fried parsnips.

He swallowed hard and tried not to look anymore. He couldn't help seeing the fried apples'n'onions, and the candied carrots. He couldn't help gazing at the triangles of pie, waiting by his plate; the spicy pumpkin pie,

the melting cream pie, the rich, dark mince oozing from between the mince pie's flaky crusts.

He squeezed his hands together between his knees. He had to sit silent and wait, but he felt aching and hollow inside.

All grown-ups at the head of the table must be served first. They were passing their plates, and talking, and heartlessly laughing. The tender pork fell away in slices under Father's carving-knife. The white breast of the goose went piece by piece from the bare breast-bone. Spoons ate up the clear cranberry jelly, and gouged deep into the mashed potatoes, and ladled away the brown gravies.

Almanzo had to wait to the very last. He was youngest of all, except Abner and the babies, and Abner was company.

At last Almanzo's plate was filled. The first taste made a pleasant feeling inside him, and it grew and grew, while he ate and ate and ate. He ate till he could eat no more, and he felt very good inside. For a while he slowly nibbled bits from his second piece of fruitcake. Then he put the fruity slice in his pocket and went out to play.

Royal and James were choosing sides, to play snow-fort. Royal chose Frank, and James chose Almanzo. When everyone was chosen, they all went to work, rolling snowballs through the deep drifts by the barn. They rolled till the balls were almost as tall as Almanzo; then they rolled them into a wall. They packed snow between them, and made a good fort.

Then each side made its own little snowballs. They breathed on the snow, and squeezed it solid. They made dozens of hard snowballs. When they were ready for the fight, Royal threw a stick into the air and caught it when it came down. James took hold of the stick above Royal's hand, then Royal took hold of it above James' hand, and so on to the end of the stick. James' hand was last, so James' side had the fort.

How the snowballs flew! Almanzo ducked and dodged and yelled, and threw snowballs as fast as he could, till they were all gone. Royal came charging over the wall with all the enemy after him, and Almanzo rose up and grabbed Frank. Headlong they went into the deep snow, outside the wall, and they rolled over and over, hitting each other as hard as they could.

Almanzo's face was covered with snow and his mouth was full of it, but he hung on to Frank and kept hitting him. Frank got him down, but Almanzo squirmed out from under. Frank's head hit his nose, and it began to bleed. Almanzo didn't care. He was on top of Frank, hitting him as

hard as he could in the deep snow. He kept saying, "Holler 'nuff! holler 'nuff!"

Frank grunted and squirmed. He rolled half over, and Almanzo got on top of him. He couldn't stay on top of Frank and hit him, so he bore down with all his weight, and he pushed Frank's face deeper and deeper into the snow. And Frank gasped: "'Nuff!"

Almanzo got up on his knees, and he saw Mother in the doorway of the house. She called:

"Boys! Boys! Stop playing now. It's time to come in and warm."

They were warm. They were hot and panting. But Mother and the aunts thought the cousins must get warm before they rode home in the cold. They all went tramping in, covered with snow, and Mother held up her hands and exclaimed:

"Mercy on us!"

The grown-ups were in the parlor, but the boys had to stay in the dining-room, so they wouldn't melt on the parlor carpet. They couldn't sit down, because the chairs were covered with blankets and laprobes, warming by the heater. But they ate apples and drank cider, standing around, and Almanzo and Abner went into the pantry and ate bits off the platters.

Then uncles and aunts and the girl cousins put on their wraps, and they brought the sleeping babies from the bedroom, rolled up in shawls. The sleighs came jingling from the barn, and Father and Mother helped tuck in the blankets and laprobes, over the hoopskirts. Everybody called: "Good-by! Good-by!"

The music of the sleigh-bells came back for a little while; then it was gone. Christmas was over.

CHRISTMAS BY THE SHORES OF SILVER LAKE

Large, soft snowflakes are falling in the Dakota territory, and Laura and her family are living in the surveyors' house by the lake for the winter. Mary is blind now, having been struck with scarlet fever. Laura and Mary are becoming young ladies, Carrie is growing bigger by the day, and there is even a new Ingalls sister, Baby Grace. The Ingallses don't have much money this year, but they would never let that stop them from celebrating the magical spirit of the Christmas season. There are special gifts to be made, Christmas carols to sing, and even new Christmas traditions to start!

Christmas Eve

It had snowed all day and soft, large flakes were still falling. The winds were quiet so that the snow lay deep on the ground, and Pa took the shovel with him when he went to do the evening chores.

"Well, it's a white Christmas," he said.

"Yes, and we're all here and all well, so it's a merry one," said Ma.

The surveyors' house was full of secrets. Mary had knitted new, warm socks for Pa's Christmas present. Laura had made him a necktie from a piece of silk she found in Ma's scrap bag. Together in the attic, she and Carrie had made an apron for Ma from one of the calico curtains that had hung in the shanty. In the scrap bag they found a piece of fine, white muslin; Laura had cut a small square from it, and secretly Mary had hemmed the square with her fine stitches and made a handkerchief for Ma. They put it in the apron pocket. Then they had wrapped the apron in tissue paper and hidden it under the quilt blocks in Mary's box.

There had been a blanket, striped across the ends in red and green. The blanket was worn out, but the striped end was good, and from it Ma had cut bed shoes for Mary. Laura had made one, and Carrie the other, seaming and turning and finishing them neatly with cords and tassels of yarn. The shoes were hidden carefully in Ma's bedroom so that Mary would not find them.

Laura and Mary had wanted to make mittens for Carrie, but they had not enough yarn. There was a little white yarn, and a little red, and a little blue, but not enough of any color to make mittens.

"I know!" Mary said. "We'll make the hands white, and the wrists in red and blue strips!" Every morning while Carrie was making her bed in the attic, Laura and Mary had knitted as fast as they could; when they heard her coming down stairs, they hid the mittens in Mary's knitting basket. The mittens were there now, finished.

Grace's Christmas present was to be the most beautiful of all. They had all worked at it together in the warm room, for Grace was so little that she didn't notice.

Ma had taken the swan's skin from its careful wrappings, and cut from it a little hood. The skin was so delicate that Ma trusted no one else to handle that; she sewed every stitch of the hood herself. But she let Laura and Carrie piece out the lining, of scraps of blue silk from the scrap bag. After Ma sewed the swan's-down hood to the lining, it would not tear.

Then Ma looked again in the scrap bag, and chose a large piece of soft blue woolen cloth, that had once been her best winter dress. Out of it she cut a little coat. Laura and Carrie sewed the seams and pressed them; Mary put the tiny stitches in the hem at the bottom. Then on the coat Ma sewed a collar of the soft swan's-down, and put narrow swan's-down cuffs on the sleeves.

The blue coat trimmed with the white swan's-down, and the delicate swan's-down hood with its lining as blue as Grace's eyes, were beautiful.

"It's like making doll's clothes," Laura said.

"Grace will be lovelier than any doll," Mary declared.

"Oh, let's put them on her now!" Carrie cried, dancing in her eagerness.

But Ma had said the coat and the hood must be laid away until Christmas, and they were. They were waiting now for tomorrow morning to come.

Pa had gone hunting. He said he intended to have the biggest jack rabbit in the territory for the Christmas dinner. And he had. At least, he had brought home the very biggest rabbit they had ever seen. Skinned and cleaned and frozen stiff, it waited now in the lean-to to be roasted tomorrow.

Pa came in from the stable, stamping the snow from his feet. He broke the ice from his mustache and spread his hands in the warmth above the stove.

"Whew!" he said. "This is a humdinger of a cold spell for the night before Christmas. It's too cold for Santa Claus to be out," and his eyes twinkled at Carrie.

"We don't need Santa Claus! We've all been—" Carrie began, then she clapped her hand over her mouth and looked quickly to see if Laura and Mary had noticed how nearly she had told secrets.

Pa turned around to warm his back in the heat from the oven, and he looked happily at them all.

"We're all snug under cover anyway," he said. "Ellen and Sam and David are warm and comfortable too, and I gave them an extra feed for Christmas Eve. Yes, it's a pretty good Christmas, isn't it, Caroline?"

"Yes, Charles, it is," said Ma. She set the bowl of hot corn meal mush on the table, and poured out the milk. "Come now, and eat. A hot supper will warm you quicker than anything else, Charles."

At supper they talked about other Christmases. They had had so many Christmases together, and here they were again, all together and warm and fed and happy. Upstairs in Laura's box there was still Charlotte, the rag doll from her Christmas stocking in the Big Woods. The tin cups and the pennies from Christmas in Indian Territory were gone now, but Laura and Mary remembered Mr. Edwards who had walked forty miles to Independence and back, to bring those presents from Santa Claus. They never had heard of Mr. Edwards since he started alone down the Verdigris

River, and they wondered what had become of him.

"Wherever he is, let's hope he's as lucky as we are," said Pa. Wherever he was, they were remembering him and wishing him happiness.

"And you're here, Pa," Laura said. "You're not lost in a blizzard." For a moment they all looked silently at Pa, thinking of that dreadful Christmas when he almost had not come home and they feared he never would.

Tears came into Ma's eyes. She tried to hide them, but she had to brush them away with her hand. They all pretended not to notice. "It's just thankfulness, Charles," Ma said, blowing her nose.

Then Pa burst out laughing. "That was the joke on me!" he said. "Starving to death for three days and nights, and eating the oyster crackers and the Christmas candy, and all the time I was under the bank of our own creek, not a hundred yards from the house!"

"I think the best Christmas was the time there was the Sunday-school Christmas tree," said Mary. "You're too little to remember, Carrie, but Oh! how wonderful that was!"

"It wasn't really as good as this one," Laura said. "Because now Carrie is old enough to remember, and now we have Grace." There was Carrie— the wolf didn't hurt her. And there on Ma's lap sat the littlest sister Grace,

with her hair the color of sunshine and eyes as blue as violets.

"Yes, this is best after all," Mary decided. "And maybe next year there'll be a Sunday-school here."

The mush was gone. Pa scraped the last drop of milk from his bowl and drank his tea. "Well," he said, "we can't have a tree, for there isn't so much as a bush on Silver Lake. We wouldn't want one anyway, just for ourselves. But we can have a little Sunday-school celebration of our own, Mary."

He went to get his fiddle box, and while Ma and Laura washed the bowls and the pot and set them away, he tuned the fiddle and rosined the bow.

Frost was thick on the windowpanes and frost furred the cracks around the door. Thickly against the clear upper edges of the windowpanes the snowflakes fluttered. But lamplight was bright on the red-and-white tablecloth, and the fire glowed behind the open drafts of the stove.

"We can't sing so soon after eating," said Pa. "So I'll just limber up the fiddle."

Merrily he played, "Away Down the River on the O-hi-o!" And, "Why Chime the Bells So Merrily." And,

> *"Jingle bells, jingle bells,*
>
> *Jingle all the way!*
>
> *Oh, what fun it is to ride,*
>
> *In a one-hoss open sleigh!"*

Then he stopped and smiled at them all. "Are you ready to sing now?"

The voice of the fiddle changed; it was going to sing a hymn. Pa played a few notes. Then they all sang:

> *"Yes, a brighter morn is breaking,*
>
> *Better days are coming on.*
>
> *All the world will be awaking*
>
> *In a new and golden dawn.*
>
> *And many nations shall come and say,*
>
> *Come, let us go up to the mountain of the Lord!*
>
> *And He will teach us, will teach us of His ways,*
>
> *And we will walk in His paths."*

The fiddle's voice wandered away, Pa seemed to be playing his thoughts to himself. But a melody grew out of them and throbbed softly until they all joined in and sang:

> *"The sun may warm the grass to life,*
>
> *The dew the drooping flower;*
>
> *And eyes grow bright and watch the light*
>
> *Of autumn's opening hour;*
>
> *But words that breathe of tenderness*
>
> *And smiles we know are true*
>
> *Are warmer than the summertime*
>
> *And brighter than the dew.*
>
> *"It is not much the world can give*
>
> *With all its subtle art;*
>
> *And gold and gems are not the things*
>
> *To satisfy the heart;*
>
> *But Oh, if those who cluster round*
>
> *The altar and the hearth,*
>
> *Have gentle words and loving smiles,*
>
> *How beautiful the earth!"*

Through the music, Mary cried out, "What's that?"

"What, Mary?" Pa asked.

"I thought I heard— Listen!" Mary said.

They listened. The lamp made a tiny purring sound, and the coals softly settled a little in the stove. Past the little space above the white frost on the windows, falling snowflakes twinkled in the lamplight shining through the glass.

"What did you think you heard, Mary?" Pa asked.

"It sounded like— There it is again!"

This time they all heard a shout. Out in the night, in the storm, a man shouted. And shouted again, quite near the house.

Ma started up. "Charles! Who on earth?"

The Night Before Christmas

Pa laid the fiddle in its box, and opened the front door quickly. Snow and cold swirled in, and again a husky shout. "Hullo-o-o, Ingalls!"

"It's Boast!" Pa cried. "Come in! Come in!" He snatched his coat and cap, jerked them on and went out into the cold.

"He must be nearly frozen!" Ma exclaimed, and she hurried to put more coal on the fire. From outside came voices and Mr. Boast's laugh.

Then the door opened and Pa called, "Here's Mrs. Boast, Caroline. We're going to put up the horses."

Mrs. Boast was a great bundle of coats and blankets. Ma hurried to help her take off layer after layer of wrappings. "Come to the stove! You must be nearly frozen."

"Oh, no," a pleasant voice answered. "The horse was warm to sit on and Robert wrapped me so tightly in all these blankets, the cold couldn't reach me. He even led the horse so my hands would be under cover."

"This veil is frozen just the same," said Ma, unwinding yards of frosted woolen veil from Mrs. Boast's head. Mrs. Boast's face appeared, framed in a fur-edged hood. Mrs. Boast did not look much older than Mary. Her hair was soft brown, and her long-lashed eyes were blue.

"Did you come all this way on horseback, Mrs. Boast?" Ma asked her.

"Oh, no. Only about two miles. We were coming in a bobsled, but we got stuck in the snow in a slough. The team and the sled fell down through the snow," she said. "Robert got the team out but we had to leave the sled."

"I know," said Ma. "The snow drifts over the top of the tall slough grass, and you can't tell where the slough is. But the grass underneath won't hold up any weight." She helped Mrs. Boast out of her coat.

"Take my chair, Mrs. Boast. It's in the warmest place," Mary urged her. But Mrs. Boast said she would sit beside Mary.

Pa and Mr. Boast came into the lean-to with a great stamping of snow from their feet. Mr. Boast laughed, and in the house everyone laughed, even Ma.

"I don't know why," Laura said to Mrs. Boast. "We don't even know what the joke is, but when Mr. Boast laughs—"

Mrs. Boast was laughing too. "It's contagious," she said. Laura looked at her blue, laughing eyes and thought that Christmas would be jolly.

Ma was stirring up biscuit. "How do you do, Mr. Boast," she said. "You and Mrs. Boast must be starved. Supper will be ready in a jiffy."

Laura put slices of salt pork in the frying pan to parboil, and Ma set the biscuits in the oven. Then Ma drained the pork, dipped the slices in flour and set them to fry, while Laura peeled and sliced potatoes.

"I'll raw-fry them," Ma said to her low, in the pantry, "and make milk gravy and a fresh pot of tea. We can make out well enough for food, but what will we do about the presents?"

Laura had not thought of that. They had no presents for Mr. and Mrs. Boast. Ma whisked out of the pantry to fry the potatoes and make the gravy, and Laura set the table.

"I don't know when I've enjoyed a meal more," said Mrs. Boast, when they had eaten.

"We didn't look for you until spring," said Pa. "Winter is a bad time to make such a drive."

"We found that out," Mr. Boast answered. "But I tell you, Ingalls, the whole country is moving west in the spring. All Iowa is coming, and we knew we must be ahead of the rush or some claim jumper would be on our homestead. So we came, weather or no weather. You should have filed on a homestead last fall. You'll have to rush it in the spring, or you'll find no land left."

Pa and Ma looked soberly at each other. They were thinking of the homestead that Pa had found. But Ma only said, "It's getting late, and Mrs. Boast must be tired."

"I am tired," Mrs. Boast said. "It was a hard drive, and then to leave the sled and come on horseback through the snowstorm. We were so glad

to see your light. And when we came nearer, we heard you singing. You don't know how good it sounded."

"You take Mrs. Boast in with you, Caroline, and Boast and I will bunk down here by the fire," Pa said. "We'll have one more song, then all you girls skedaddle."

He raised the fiddle again from its nest in the box and tried it to see that it was in tune. "What'll it be, Boast?"

"'Merry Christmas Everywhere,'" said Mr. Boast. His tenor voice joined Pa's bass. Mrs. Boast's soft alto and Laura's soprano and Mary's followed, then Ma's contralto. Carrie's little treble piped up happily.

> *"Merry, Merry Christmas everywhere!*
> *Cheerily it ringeth through the air;*
> *Christmas bells, Christmas trees,*
> *Christmas odors on the breeze.*

> *"Why should we so joyfully*
> *Sing with grateful mirth?*
> *See the Sun of Righteousness*
> *Beams upon the earth!*

34

"Light for weary wanderers,

Comfort for the oppressed;

He will guide his trusting ones,

Into perfect rest."

"Good night! Good night!" they all said. Ma came upstairs to get Carrie's bedding for Pa and Mr. Boast. "Their blankets are sopping wet," she said. "You three girls can share one bed for one night."

"Ma! What about the presents?" Laura whispered.

"Never mind, I'll manage somehow," Ma whispered back. "Now go to sleep, girls," she said aloud. "Good night, sleep tight!"

Downstairs Mrs. Boast was softly singing to herself, "Light for weary wanderers . . ."

Merry Christmas

When Laura heard the door shut as Pa and Mr. Boast went out to do the morning chores, she dressed chattering in the cold and hurried downstairs to help Ma get breakfast.

But Mrs. Boast was helping Ma. The room was warm from the glowing stove. Mush was frying on the long griddle. The teakettle was boiling and the table was set.

"Merry Christmas!" Ma and Mrs. Boast said together.

"Merry Christmas," Laura answered but she was staring at the table. At each place, the plate was turned bottom-up over the knife and fork, as usual. But on the plates' bottoms were packages, small packages and larger packages, some wrapped in colored tissue paper and others in plain wrapping paper tied with colored string.

"You see, Laura, we didn't hang up stockings last night," said Ma, "so we will take our presents off the table at breakfast."

Laura went back upstairs, and told Mary and Carrie about the Christmas breakfast table. "Ma knew where we hid all the presents but hers," she said. "They are all on the table."

"But we can't have presents!" Mary wailed horrified. "There isn't anything for Mr. and Mrs. Boast!"

"Ma will fix it," Laura answered. "She told me so last night."

"How can she?" Mary asked. "We didn't know they were coming! There isn't anything we could give them."

"Ma can fix anything," said Laura. She took Ma's present from Mary's box and held it behind her when they all went downstairs together. Carrie stood between her and Ma while quickly Laura put the package on Ma's plate. There was a little package on Mrs. Boast's plate, and another on Mr. Boast's.

"Oh, I can't wait!" Carrie whispered, squeezing her thin hands

together. Her peaked face was white and her eyes were big and shining.

"Yes, you can. We've got to," said Laura. It was easier for Grace, who was so little that she did not notice the Christmas table. But even Grace was so excited that Mary could hardly button her up.

"Mewy Cwismas! Mewy Cwismas!" Grace shouted, wriggling, and when she was free she ran about, shouting, until Ma told her gently that children must be seen and not heard.

"Come here, Grace, and you can see out," said Carrie. She had blown and wiped a clear space in the frost on the windowpane, and there they stayed, taking turns at looking out, till at last Carrie said, "Here they come!"

After a loud stamping-off of snow in the lean-to, Pa and Mr. Boast came in.

"Merry Christmas! Merry Christmas!" they all cried.

Grace ran behind Ma and clung to her skirts, peeping around them at the strange man. Pa picked her up and tossed her, just as he used to toss Laura when Laura was little. And Graced screamed with laughter just as Laura used to. Laura had to remember hard that she was a big girl now or she would have laughed out loud too. They were all so happy in the warmth full of good smells of cooking, and with company there for Christmas in the snug house. The light from the frost-furred windows was silvery, and just as they all sat down to that exciting Christmas table, the eastern window turned golden; outdoors the stillness of the whole vast snowy prairie was full of sunshine.

"You first, Mrs. Boast," said Ma, for Mrs. Boast was company. So Mrs. Boast opened her package. In it was a lawn handkerchief edged with narrow crocheted lace. Laura recognized it; it was Ma's best Sunday hand-kerchief. Mrs. Boast was delighted, and so surprised that there was a gift for her.

So was Mr. Boast. His present was wristlets, knitted in stripes of red and gray. They fitted him perfectly. They were the wristlets that Ma had knitted for Pa. But she could knit some more for Pa, and the company must have Christmas presents.

Pa said his new socks were exactly what he needed; the cold from the snow had been going right through his boots. And he admired the necktie that Laura had made. "I'll put this on, right after breakfast!" he said. "By George, now I'll be all dressed up for Christmas!"

Everyone exclaimed when Ma unwrapped her pretty apron. She put it

on at once, and stood up for them all to see. She looked at the hem, and smiled at Carrie. "You hem very nicely, Carrie," she said, then she smiled at Laura, "And Laura's gathers are even, and well sewed. It is a nice apron."

"There's more, Ma!" Carrie cried out. "Look in the pocket!"

Ma took out the handkerchief. She was so surprised. And to think that the very morning she gave away her Sunday best handkerchief, she was given another one; it was as if this had been planned, though none of them had planned it. But of course this could not be said in Mrs. Boast's hearing. Ma only looked at the handkerchief's tiny hem and said, "Such a pretty handkerchief too! Thank you, Mary."

Then everyone admired Mary's bed shoes, and how they had been made of the ends of a worn-out blanket. Mrs. Boast said she was going to make some for herself, as soon as any of her blankets wore out.

Carrie put on her mittens and softly clapped her hands. "My Fourth of July mittens! Oh, see my Fourth of July mittens!" she said.

Then Laura opened her package. And in it was an apron, made of the same calico as Ma's! It was smaller than Ma's apron, and had two pockets. A narrow ruffle was all around it. Ma had cut it out of the other curtain,

Carrie had sewed all the seams, Mary had hemmed the ruffle. All that time, Ma hadn't known and Laura hadn't known that each was making an apron for the other from those old curtains, and Mary and Carrie had been almost bursting with the two secrets.

"Oh, thank you! Thank you all!" Laura said, smoothing down the pretty white calico with the little red flowers scattered over it. "Such tiny stitches in the ruffle, Mary! I do thank you."

Then came the best part of all. Everyone watched while Ma put the little blue coat on Grace and smoothed the swan's-down collar. She put the lovely white swan's-down hood over Grace's golden hair. A bit of the blue silk lining showed around Grace's face and matched her shining eyes. She touched the fluffy soft swan's-down on her wrists, and waved her hands and laughed.

She was so beautiful and so happy, blue and white and gold and alive and laughing, that they could not look at her long enough. But Ma did not want to spoil her with too much attention. So, too soon, she quieted Grace and laid away the coat and hood in the bedroom.

There was still another package beside Laura's plate, and she saw that Mary and Carrie and Grace each had one like it. All at once, they unwrapped them, and each found a little pink cheesecloth bag full of candy.

"Christmas candy!" Carrie cried and "Christmas candy!" Laura and Mary said at the same time.

"However did Christmas candy get here?" Mary asked.

"Why, didn't Santa Claus get here on Christmas Eve?" said Pa. So, almost all at once, they said, "Oh, Mr. Boast! Thank you! Thank you, Mr. and Mrs. Boast!"

Then Laura gathered up all the paper wrappings, and she helped Ma set on the table the big platter of golden, fried mush, a plate of hot biscuits, a dish of fried potatoes, a bowl of codfish gravy and a glass dish full of dried-apple sauce.

"I'm sorry we have no butter," said Ma. "Our cow gives so little milk that we can't make butter anymore."

But the codfish gravy was good on the mush and the potatoes, and nothing could taste better than hot biscuits and applesauce. Such a breakfast as that, like Christmas, came only once a year. And there was still the Christmas dinner to come, on that same day.

After breakfast, Pa and Mr. Boast went with the team to get Mr.

Boast's bobsled. They took shovels to dig the snow away so that horses could pull it out of the slough.

Then Mary took Grace on her lap in the rocking chair, and while Carrie made the beds and swept, Ma and Laura and Mrs. Boast put on their aprons, rolled up their sleeves, and washed the dishes and got dinner.

Mrs. Boast was great fun. She was interested in everything, and eager to learn how Ma managed so well.

"When you haven't milk enough to have sour milk, however do you make such delicious biscuits, Laura?" she asked.

"Why, you just use sour dough," Laura said.

Mrs. Boast had never made sour-dough biscuits! It was fun to show her. Laura measured out the cups of sour dough, put in the soda and salt and flour, and rolled out the biscuits on the board.

"But how do you make the sour dough?" Mrs. Boast asked.

"You start it," said Ma, "by putting some flour and warm water in a jar and letting it stand till it sours."

"Then when you use it, always leave a little," said Laura. "And put in the scraps of biscuit dough, like this, and more warm water," Laura put in the warm water, "and cover it," she put the clean cloth and the plate on the jar, "and just set it in a warm place," she set it in its place on the shelf by the stove. "And it's always ready to use, whenever you want it."

"I never tasted better biscuits," said Mrs. Boast.

With such good company, the morning seemed to go in a minute. Dinner was almost ready when Pa and Mr. Boast came back with the bob-sled. The enormous jack rabbit was browning in the oven. Potatoes were boiling, and the coffee pot bubbled on the back of the stove. The house was full of the good smells of roasting meat, hot breads, and coffee. Pa sniffed when he came in.

"Don't worry, Charles," said Ma. "You smell coffee, but the kettle is boiling to make your tea."

"Good! Tea is a man's drink in cold weather," Pa told her.

Laura spread the clean white tablecloth, and in the center of the table she set the glass sugar bowl, the glass pitcher full of cream, and the glass spoonholder full of silver spoons all standing on their handles. Around the table Carrie laid the knives and forks, and filled the water glasses, while Laura set all the plates in a pile at Pa's place. Then at each place, all around the table, she cheerfully put a glass sauce dish holding half a canned peach in golden syrup. The table was beautiful.

Pa and Mr. Boast had washed and combed their hair. Ma put the last empty pot and pan in the pantry, and helped Laura and Mrs. Boast whisk the last full dish to the table. Quickly she and Laura took off their work aprons and tied on their Christmas aprons.

"Come!" said Ma. "Dinner is ready."

"Come, Boast!" said Pa. "Sit up and eat hearty! There's plenty more down cellar in a teacup!"

Before Pa, on the big platter, lay the huge roasted rabbit with piles of bread-and-onion stuffing steaming around it. From a dish on one side stood up a mound of mashed potatoes, and on the other side stood a bowl of rich, brown gravy.

There were plates of hot Johnny cake and of small hot biscuits. There was a dish of cucumber pickles.

Ma poured the strong brown coffee and the fragrant tea, while Pa heaped each plate with roast rabbit, stuffing, and potatoes and gravy.

"This is the first time we ever had jack rabbit for Christmas dinner," Pa said. "The other time we lived where jack rabbits grow, they were too common, we had them every day. For Christmas we had wild turkey."

"Yes, Charles, and that was the most we did have," said Ma. "There was

no surveyors' pantry to get pickles and peaches out of, in Indian Territory."

"Seems to me this is the best rabbit I ever tasted," said Mr. Boast. "The gravy is extra good too."

"Hunger is the best sauce," Ma replied modestly. But Mrs. Boast said, "I know why the rabbit's so good. Mrs. Ingalls lays thin slices of salt pork over it when she roasts it."

"Why, yes, I do," Ma agreed. "I think it does improve the flavor."

They all took big second helpings. Then Pa and Mr. Boast took big third helpings, and Mary and Laura and Carrie did not refuse, but Ma took only a bit of stuffing and Mrs. Boast just one more biscuit. "I declare, I'm so full I can't eat another mouthful," she said.

When Pa took up the fork from the platter again, Ma warned him. "Save some room, Charles, you and Mr. Boast."

"You don't mean there's more to come?" said Pa.

Then Ma stepped into the pantry and brought out the dried-apple pie.

"Pie!" said Pa, and, "Apple pie!" said Mr. Boast. "Jumping Jehoshaphat, I wish I'd known this was coming!"

Slowly they each ate a piece of that apple pie, and Pa and Mr. Boast divided the one piece left over.

"I never hope to eat a better Christmas dinner," said Mr. Boast, with a deep sigh of fullness.

"Well," Pa said. "It's the first Christmas dinner anybody ever ate in this part of the country. I'm glad it was a good one. In time to come, no doubt a good many folks will celebrate Christmas around here, and I expect they'll have fancier fixings in some ways, but I don't know how they can have more solid comfort than we've got, for a fact."

After a while he and Mr. Boast got up reluctantly, and Ma began to clear the table. "I'll do the dishes," she said to Laura. "You run help Mrs. Boast get settled."

So Laura and Mrs. Boast put on their coats and hoods, mufflers and mittens, and went out into the glittering, biting cold. Laughing, they plowed and plunged through snow, to the tiny house nearby that had been the surveyors' office. At its door Pa and Mr. Boast unloaded the bobsled.

The little house had no floor, and it was so small that the double bedstead just fitted across one end. In the corner by the door Pa and Mr. Boast set up the stove. Laura helped Mrs. Boast carry the feather bed and quilts and make the bed. Then they set the table against the window opposite the stove, and pushed two chairs under it. Mrs. Boast's trunk

squeezed between the table and the bed and made another seat. A shelf above the stove and a box beside it held the dishes, and just room enough was left for the door to open against the table.

"There!" Pa said, when all was done. "Now you folks are settled, come on over. Not even the four of us can get in here, but there's plenty of room at the other house, so that's headquarters. How about a game of checkers, Boast?"

"You go along," Mrs. Boast told them. "Laura and I will come in a minute."

When they were gone, Mrs. Boast took a full paper bag from under the dishes. "It's for a surprise," she told Laura. "Popcorn! Rob doesn't know I brought it."

They smuggled the bag into the house and hid it in the pantry, whispering to tell Ma what it was. And later, when Pa and Mr. Boast were absorbed in checkers, quietly they heated fat in the iron kettle and poured in a handful of the shelled popcorn. At the first crackle, Pa looked around quickly.

"Popcorn!" he exclaimed. "I haven't tasted popcorn since— If I'd known you'd brought popcorn, Boast, I'd have routed it out before now."

"I didn't bring popcorn," said Mr. Boast. Then he cried out, "Nell, you rascal!"

"You two go on with your game!" Mrs. Boast told him, laughing at him with her blue eyes. "You're much too busy to notice us."

"Yes, Charles," said Ma. "Don't let us disturb your checkers."

"I've got you beat anyway, Boast," said Pa.

"Not yet you haven't," Mr. Boast contradicted.

Ma dipped the snowy kernels from the kettle into a milkpan, and Laura carefully salted them. They popped another kettleful, and the pan would hold no more. Then Mary and Laura and Carrie had a plateful of the crispy crackly melting-soft corn, and Pa and Ma and Mr. and Mrs. Boast sat around the pan, eating and talking and laughing, till chore-time and suppertime and the time when Pa would play the fiddle.

"Every Christmas is better than the Christmas before," Laura thought. "I guess it must be because I'm growing up."

CHRISTMAS DURING THE LONG WINTER

The Ingallses are living in De Smet, and this year the blizzards are relentless. There has been so much snow, the trains can't make their way into town. As Christmas Day approaches, Laura and her sisters wonder what Christmas will be like without the gifts and delicious foods the trains were bound to deliver.

When the long winter finally comes to an end, Laura and her family decide to celebrate the welcome arrival of spring in a very special way.

Merry Christmas

The blizzard stopped at last. After three days of its ceaseless noise, the stillness rang in Laura's ears.

Pa hurried away to get a load of hay and when he came back he put David in the stable. The sun was still glittering on the snow, there was no cloud in the northwest, and Laura wondered why he stopped hauling hay.

"What's wrong, Charles?" Ma asked quietly when Pa came in.

Pa answered, "Gilbert made it to Preston and back. He's brought the mail!"

It was as if Christmas had happened unexpectedly. Ma hoped for the

church paper. Laura and Mary and Carrie hoped that Reverend Alden had sent them something to read; sometimes he did. Grace was excited because they were excited. It was hard to wait for Pa to come back from the post office.

He was gone a long time. As Ma said, it did no good to be impatient. Every man in town was at the post office and Pa must wait his turn.

When at last he came, his hands were full. Ma reached eagerly for the church papers and Laura and Carrie both tried to take the bundle of *Youth's Companion*s. There were newspapers too.

"Here! Here!" Pa laughed. "Don't mob a fellow! And that's not the whole of it. Guess what I got!"

"A letter? Oh Pa, did you get a letter?" Laura cried.

"Who is it from?" Ma asked.

"You've got the *Advance*s, Caroline," Pa replied. "And Laura and Carrie've got the *Youth's Companion*s. I've got the *Inter-Ocean* and the *Pioneer Press*. Mary gets the letter."

Mary's face shone. She felt the letter's size and thickness. "A big, fat letter! Please read it, Ma."

So Ma opened the letter and read it aloud.

The letter was from Reverend Alden. He was sorry that he had not been able to come back and help organize a church last spring, but he had been sent farther north. He hoped to be with them when spring came again. The children of the Sunday School in Minnesota were sending a bundle of *Youth's Companion*s to the girls, and would send another bundle next year. His church had shipped them a Christmas barrel and he hoped the clothing would fit. As his own Christmas gift and some slight return for their hospitality to him and to Reverend Stuart last winter at Silver Lake, he had put in a Christmas turkey. He wished them all a Merry Christmas and a Happy New Year.

There was a little silence when Ma had finished reading. Then she said, "We have this good letter, anyway."

"Gilbert brought word that they're putting on a double work crew and two snowplows at the Tracy cut," Pa told them. "We may get the barrel by Christmas."

"It's only a few days," Ma said.

"A lot can be done in a few days," said Pa. "If this spell of clear weather holds out, no reason they can't get the train through."

"Oh, I hope the Christmas barrel comes," Carrie said.

"The hotels have shut down," Pa told Ma the news. "They've been burning lumber and now Banker Ruth has bought out the lumberyard, down to the last shingle."

"We couldn't afford to burn lumber anyway," said Ma. "But Charles, we are almost out of coal."

"We'll burn hay," Pa answered cheerfully.

"Hay?" Ma said, and Laura asked, "How can we burn hay, Pa?"

She thought of how quickly the prairie fires swept through dry grass. Flame licks through the light, thin stems and is gone before the frail ashes can fall. How could a room be kept warm by a fire so quickly burning out, when even the steady glow of hard coal could not keep out the cold?

"We will have to contrive," Pa told her. "We'll manage it! Needs must, when the devil drives."

"Likely the train will get through in time," Ma said.

Pa put on his cap again and asked Ma to make dinner a little late. He had time to haul another load of hay if he hustled. He went out and Ma said, "Come, girls, put the bundle of *Youth's Companion*s away. We must get out the washing while the weather's clear so we can."

All that day Laura and Carrie and Mary looked forward to the *Youth's*

*Companion*s and often they spoke of them. But the bright day was short. They stirred and punched the clothes boiling on the stove; they lifted them on the broom handle into the tub where Ma soaped and rubbed them. Laura rinsed them, Carrie stirred the blueing bag in the second rinse-water until it was blue enough. Laura made the boiled starch. And when for the last time Ma went out into the cold to hang the freezing wash on the line, Pa had come for dinner.

Then they washed the dishes, they scrubbed the floor and blacked the stove, and washed the inside of the windowpanes. Ma brought in the frozen-dry clothes and they sorted them and sprinkled them and rolled them tightly, ready for ironing. Twilight had come. It was too late to read that day and after supper there was no lamplight because they must save the last of the kerosene.

"Work comes before pleasure," Ma always said. She smiled her gentle smile for Laura and Carrie and said now, "My girls have helped me do a good day's work," and they were rewarded.

"Tomorrow we'll read a story," Carrie said happily.

"Tomorrow we have to do the ironing," Laura reminded her.

"Yes, and we should air the bedding and give the upstairs a thorough

cleaning, in this good weather," said Ma.

Pa came in and heard them. "Tomorrow I'm going to work on the railroad," he said.

Mr. Woodworth had word to put at work on the tracks all the men he could get. The superintendent at the Tracy cut was driving the work there and shovel gangs were shoveling eastward from Huron.

"If muscle and will-power can do it, we'll have a train through by Christmas!" Pa declared.

That night he came back from work with a broad smile on his sun-red face. "Good news!" he called out. "The work train will come through sometime tomorrow! The regular train'll come next, day after tomorrow probably."

"Oh, good! Good! Goody!" Laura and Carrie exclaimed together, and Ma said, "That is good news, indeed. What is wrong with your eyes, Charles?"

His eyes were red and puffed. He answered cheerfully, "Shoveling snow in the sunshine is hard on eyes. Some of the men are snow-blind. Fix me up a little weak salt-water, will you, Caroline? And I'll bathe them after I do the chores."

When he had gone to the stable, Ma dropped into a chair near Mary. "I'm afraid, girls, this will be a poor Christmas," she said. "What with these awful storms and trying to keep warm, we've had no time to plan for it."

"Maybe the Christmas barrel . . ." Carrie began.

"We mustn't count on it," said Mary.

"We could wait for Christmas till it comes," Laura suggested. "All but . . ." and she picked up Grace who was listening wide-eyed.

"Can't Santa Claus come?" Grace asked, and her lower lip began to tremble.

Laura hugged her and looked over her golden head at Ma.

Ma said firmly, "Santa Claus always comes to good little girls, Grace. But girls," she went on, "I have an idea. What do you think of saving my church papers and your bundle of *Youth's Companion*s to open on Christmas day?"

After a moment Mary said, "I think it is a good idea. It will help us to learn self-denial."

"I don't want to," Laura said.

"Nobody does," said Mary. "But it's good for us."

Sometimes Laura did not even want to be good. But after another silent moment she said, "Well, if you and Mary want to, Ma, I will. It will give us something to look forward to for Christmas."

"What do you say about it, Carrie?" Ma asked, and in a small voice Carrie said, "I will, too, Ma."

"That's my good girls," Ma approved them. She went on. "We can find a little something in the stores for . . ." and she glanced at Grace. "But you older girls know, Pa hasn't been able to get any work for wages this year.

We can't spare money for presents, but we can have a happy Christmas just the same. I'll try to contrive something extra for dinner and then we'll all open our papers and read them, and when it's too dark to read, Pa will play the fiddle."

"We haven't much flour left, Ma," Laura said.

"The storekeepers are asking twenty-five cents a pound for flour so Pa's waiting for the train," Ma replied. "There's nothing to make a pie, anyway, and no butter or eggs for a cake and no more sugar in town. But we'll think of something for Christmas dinner."

Laura sat thinking. She was making a little picture frame of cross-stitch in wools on thin, silver-colored cardboard. Up the sides and across the top she had made a pattern of small blue flowers and green leaves. Now she was outlining the picture-opening in blue. While she put the tiny needle through the perforations in the cardboard and drew the fine, colored wool carefully after it, she was thinking how wistfully Carrie had looked at the beautiful thing. She decided to give it to Carrie for Christmas. Someday, perhaps, she could make another for herself.

How fortunate it was that she had finished knitting the lace for her petticoat. She would give that to Mary. And to Ma she would give the

cardboard hair receiver that she had already embroidered to match the picture frame. Ma could hang it on the corner of her looking glass, and when she combed her hair she would put the combings in it to use later in the hair-switch she was making.

"But what can we do for Pa?" she asked.

"I declare I don't know," Ma worried. "I can't think of a thing."

"I've got some pennies," Carrie said.

"There's my college money," Mary began, but Ma said, "No, Mary, we won't touch that."

"I have ten cents," Laura said thoughtfully. "How many pennies have you, Carrie?"

"I have five," Carrie told her.

"We'd need twenty-five to get Pa a pair of suspenders," Laura said. "He needs a new pair."

"I have a dime," said Ma. "So that is settled. Laura, you and Carrie had better go and buy them as soon as Pa has gone to work tomorrow morning."

Next day, when their morning work was done, Laura and Carrie crossed the snowy street to Mr. Harthorn's store. Mr. Harthorn was there alone and the shelves were bare. On both long walls there were only a few pairs of men's boots and women's shoes and some bolts of calico.

The bean barrel was empty. The cracker barrel was empty. The little brine in the bottom of the pork barrel had no pork in it. The long, flat codfish box held only a little salt scattered on its bottom. The dried-apple box and the dried-blackberry box were empty.

"I'm sold out of groceries till the train gets here," Mr. Harthorn said. "I was expecting a bill of groceries when the train stopped."

Some pretty handkerchiefs, combs, and hairpins, and two pairs of suspenders were in the showcase. Laura and Carrie looked at the suspenders. They were plain, dull gray.

"Shall I do them up for you?" Mr. Harthorn asked.

Laura did not like to say no, but she looked at Carrie and saw that Carrie hoped she would.

"No, thank you, Mr. Harthorn," Laura said. "We will not take them now."

Out in the glittering cold again, she said to Carrie, "Let's go to Loftus' store and see if we can't find prettier ones."

They bent their heads against the strong, cold wind and struggled

along the icy path on the store porches till they reached the other Dry Goods and Groceries.

That store was bare and echoing, too. Every barrel and box was empty, and where the canned goods had been there were only two flat cans of oysters.

"I'm expecting a stock of groceries when the train comes tomorrow," Mr. Loftus told them. "It won't get here any too soon either."

In his showcase was a pair of blue suspenders, with small red flowers beautifully machine-woven along them, and bright brass buckles. Laura had never seen such pretty suspenders. They were just right for Pa.

"How much are they?" she asked, almost sure that they would cost too much. But the price was twenty-five cents. Laura gave Mr. Loftus her own two five-cent pieces, Carrie's five pennies, and Ma's thin silver ten-cent piece. She took the slim package and the wind blew her and Carrie breathlessly home.

At bedtime that night no one spoke of hanging up stockings. Grace was too young to know about hanging stockings on Christmas Eve and no one else expected a present. But they had never been so eager for Christmas Day, because the tracks were clear now and the train would come tomorrow.

Laura's first thought in the morning was, "The train is coming today!" The window was not frosted, the sky was clear, the snowy prairie was turning rosy in early sunshine. The train would surely come and joyfully Laura thought about her Christmas surprises.

She slid out of bed without waking Mary and quickly pulled on her dress in the cold. She opened the box where she kept her own things. She took out the roll of knitted lace, already wrapped carefully in tissue paper. Then she found the prettiest card she had ever been given in Sunday school and she took the little embroidered picture frame and the cardboard hair receiver. With these in her hands, she hurried tiptoe downstairs.

Ma looked up in surprise. The table was set and Ma was putting on each plate a little package wrapped in red-and-white striped paper.

"Merry Christmas, Ma!" Laura whispered. "Oh, what are they?"

"Christmas presents," Ma whispered. "Whatever have you got there?"

Laura only smiled. She put her packages at Ma's plate and Mary's. Then she slipped the Sunday school card into the embroidered frame. "For Carrie," she whispered. She and Ma looked at it; it was beautiful. Then Ma found a piece of tissue paper to wrap it in.

Carrie and Grace and Mary were already clambering down the stairs, calling, "Merry Christmas! Merry Christmas!"

"Oo-oo!" Carrie squealed. "I thought we were waiting for Christmas till the Christmas barrel came on the train! Oo-oo, look! look!"

"What is it?" Mary asked.

"There are presents at every plate on the table!" Carrie told her.

"No, no, Grace, mustn't touch," Ma said. "We will all wait for Pa." So Grace ran around the table, looking but not touching.

Pa came with the milk and Ma strained it. Then Pa stepped into the lean-to and came back grinning broadly. He handed Ma the two cans of oysters from Loftus' store.

"Charles!" Ma said.

"Make us an oyster soup for Christmas dinner, Caroline!" Pa told her. "I got some milk from Ellen, not much, and it's the last; she's as good as dry. But maybe you can make it do."

"I'll thin it out with water," said Ma. "We'll have oyster soup for Christmas dinner!"

Then Pa saw the table. Laura and Carrie laughed aloud, shouting, "Merry Christmas, Merry Christmas, Pa!" and Laura told Mary, "Pa's surprised!"

"Hurrah for Santa Claus!" Pa sang out. "The old fellow made it in, if the train didn't!"

They all sat down at their places, and Ma gently held back Grace's hands. "Pa opens his first, Grace," she said.

Pa picked up his package. "Now what can this be, and who gave it to me?" He untied the string, unfolded the paper, and held up the new red-flowered suspenders.

"Whew!" he exclaimed. "Now how am I ever going to wear my coat? These are too fine to cover up." He looked around at all the faces. "All of you did this," he said. "Well, I'll be proud to wear them!"

"Not yet, Grace," Ma said. "Mary is next."

Mary unwrapped the yards of fine knitted lace. She fingered it lovingly and her face was shining with delight. "I'll save it to wear when I go to college," she said. "It's another thing to help me to go. It will be so pretty on a white petticoat."

Carrie was looking at her present. The picture was of the Good Shepherd in His blue and white robes, holding in His arms a snow-white lamb. The silvery cardboard embroidered in blue flowers made a perfect frame for it.

"Oh, how lovely. How lovely," Carrie whispered.

Ma said the hair receiver was just what she had been needing.

Then Grace tore the paper from her gift and gave a gurgle of joy. Two little, flat wooden men stood on a platform between two flat red posts. Their hands held on to two strings twisted tightly together above their heads. They wore peaked red caps and blue coats with gold buttons. Their trousers were red-and-green stripes. Their boots were black with turned-up toes.

Ma gently pressed the bottoms of the posts inward. One of the men somersaulted up and the other swung into his place. Then the first came down while the second went up and they nodded their heads and jerked their arms and swung their legs, dancing and somersaulting.

"Oh, look! Oh, look!" Grace shouted. She could never have enough of watching the funny little men dancing.

The small striped packages at each place held Christmas candy.

"Wherever did you get candy, Pa?" Laura wondered.

"I got it some time ago. It was the last bit of sugar in town," said Pa. "Some folks said they'd use it for sugar, but I made sure of our Christmas candy."

"Oh, what a lovely Christmas," Carrie sighed. Laura thought so too. Whatever happened, they could always have a merry Christmas. And the sun was shining, the sky was blue, the railroad tracks were clear, and the train was coming. The train had come through the Tracy cut that morning. Sometime that day they would hear its whistle and see it stopping by the depot.

At noon Ma was making the oyster soup. Laura was setting the table, Carrie and Grace were playing with the jumping-jack. Ma tasted the soup and set the kettle back on the stove. "The oysters are ready," she said, and stooping she looked at the slices of bread toasting in the oven. "And the bread is toasted. Whatever is Pa doing?"

"He's bringing in hay," said Laura.

Pa opened the door. Behind him the lean-to was almost full of slough hay. He asked, "Is the oyster soup ready?"

"I'm taking it up," Ma replied. "I'm glad the train is coming, this is the last of the coal." Then she looked at Pa and asked, "What is wrong, Charles?"

Pa said slowly, "There is a cloud in the northwest."

"Oh, not another blizzard!" Ma cried.

"I'm afraid so," Pa answered. "But it needn't spoil our dinner." He drew his chair up to the table. "I've packed plenty of hay into the stable and filled the lean-to. Now for our oyster soup!"

The sun kept on shining while they ate. The hot soup was good, even though the milk was mostly water. Pa crumbled the toast into his soup plate. "This toasted bread is every bit as good as crackers," he told Ma. "I don't know but better."

Laura enjoyed the good soup, but she could not stop thinking of that dark cloud coming up. She could not stop listening for the wind that she knew would soon come.

It came with a shriek. The windows rattled and the house shook.

"She must be a daisy!" Pa said. He went to the window but he could not see out. Snow came on the wind from the sky. Snow rose from the hard drifts as the wind cut them away. It all met in the whirling air and swirled madly. The sky, the sunshine, the town, were gone, lost in that blinding dance of snow. The house was alone again.

Laura thought, "The train can't come now."

"Come, girls," Ma said. "We'll get these dishes out of the way, and then we'll open our papers and have a cosy afternoon."

"Is there coal enough, Ma?" Laura asked.

Pa looked at the fire. "It will last till suppertime," he said. "And then we'll burn hay."

Frost was freezing up the windowpanes and the room was cold near the walls. Near the stove, the light was too dim for reading. When the dishes were washed and put away, Ma set the lamp on the red-checked tablecloth and lighted it. There was only a little kerosene in the bowl where the wick coiled, but it gave a warm and cheery light. Laura opened the bundle of *Youth's Companion*s and she and Carrie looked eagerly at the wealth of stories printed on the smooth white paper.

"You girls choose a story," Ma said. "And I will read it out loud, so we can all enjoy it together."

So, close together between the stove and the bright table, they listened to Ma's reading the story in her soft, clear voice. The story took them all far away from the stormy cold and dark. When she had finished that one, Ma read a second and a third. That was enough for one day; they must save some for another time.

"Aren't you glad we saved those wonderful stories for Christmas day?" Mary sighed happily. And they were. The whole afternoon had gone so quickly. Already it was chore time.

When Pa came back from the stable, he stayed some time in the lean-to and came in at last with his arms full of sticks.

"Here is your breakfast fuel, Caroline," he said, laying his armful down by the stove. "Good hard sticks of hay. I guess they will burn all right."

"Sticks of hay?" Laura exclaimed.

"That's right, Laura." Pa spread his hands in the warmth above the stove. "I'm glad that hay's in the lean-to. I couldn't carry it in through the wind that's blowing now, unless I brought it one bale at a time, in my teeth."

The hay was in sticks. Pa had somehow twisted and knotted it tightly till each stick was almost as hard as wood.

"Sticks of hay!" Ma laughed. "What won't you think of next? Trust you, Charles, to find a way."

"You are good at that yourself," Pa smiled at her.

For supper there were hot boiled potatoes and a slice of bread apiece, with salt. That was the last baking of bread, but there were still beans in the sack and a few turnips. There was still hot tea with sugar, and Grace had her cup of cambric tea made with hot water because there was no more milk. While they were eating, the lamp began to flicker. With all its might the flame pulled itself up, drawing the last drop of kerosene up the wick. Then it fainted down and desperately tried again. Ma leaned over and blew it out. The dark came in, loud with the roar and the shrieking of the storm.

"The fire is dying, anyway, so we may as well go to bed," Ma said gently. Christmas Day was over.

Laura lay in bed and listened to the winds blowing, louder and louder. They sounded like the pack of wolves howling around the little house on the prairie long ago, when she was small and Pa had carried her in his arms. And there was the deeper howl of the great buffalo wolf that she and Carrie had met on the bank of Silver Lake.

She started trembling, when she heard the scream of the panther in the creek bed, in Indian territory. But she knew it was only the wind. Now she heard the Indian war whoops when the Indians were dancing their war dances all through the horrible nights by the Verdigris River.

The war whoops died away and she heard crowds of people muttering, then shrieking and fleeing screaming away from fierce yells chasing them. But she knew she heard only the voices of the blizzard winds. She pulled the bedcovers over her head and covered her ears tightly to shut out the sounds, but still she heard them.

The Christmas Barrel

The following May, after the long winter months, the trains finally made their way into town. After the second train's departing whistle had died away, Pa and Mr. Boast came down the street carrying a barrel between them. They upended it through the doorway and stood it in the middle of the front room.

"Here's that Christmas barrel!" Pa called to Ma.

He brought his hammer and began pulling nails out of the barrel-head, while they all stood around it waiting to see what was in it. Pa took off the barrel-head. Then he lifted away some thick brown paper that covered everything beneath.

Clothes were on top. First Pa drew out a dress of beautifully fine, dark-blue flannel. The skirt was full pleated and the neat, whaleboned basque was buttoned down the front with cut-steel buttons.

"This is about your size, Caroline," Pa beamed. "Here, take it!" and he reached again into the barrel.

He took out a fluffy, light-blue fascinator for Mary, and some warm flannel underthings. He took out a pair of black leather shoes that exactly fitted Laura. He took out five pairs of white woolen stockings, machine-knit. They were much finer and thinner than home-knit ones.

Then he took out a warm, brown coat, a little large for Carrie, but it would fit her next winter. And he took out a red hood and mittens to go with it.

Next came a silk shawl!

"Oh, Mary!" Laura said. "The most beautiful thing—a shawl made of silk! It is dove-colored, with fine stripes of green and rose and black and the richest, deep fringe with all those colors shimmering in it. Feel how soft and rich and heavy the silk is," and she put a corner of the shawl in Mary's hand.

"Oh, lovely!" Mary breathed.

"Who gets this shawl?" Pa asked, and they all said, "Ma!" Such a beautiful shawl was for Ma, of course. Pa laid it on her arm, and it was like her, so soft and yet firm and well-wearing, with the fine, bright colors in it.

"We will all take turns wearing it," Ma said. "And Mary shall take it with her when she goes to college."

"What is there for you, Pa?" Laura asked jealously. For Pa there were two fine, white shirts, and a dark brown plush cap.

"That isn't all," said Pa, and he lifted out of the barrel one, two little dresses. One was blue flannel, one was green-and-rose plaid. They were too small for Carrie and too big for Grace, but Grace would grow to fit them. Then were was an A-B-C book printed on cloth, and a small, shiny Mother Goose book of the smoothest paper, with a colored picture on the cover.

There was a pasteboard box full of bright-colored yarns and another box filled with embroidery silks and sheets of perforated thin cardboard, silver-colored and gold-colored. Ma gave both boxes to Laura, saying, "You gave away the pretty things you had made. Now here are some lovely things for you to work with."

Laura was so happy that she couldn't say a word. The delicate silks caught on the roughness of her fingers, scarred from twisting hay, but the beautiful colors sang together like music, and her fingers would grow smooth again so that she could embroider on the fine, thin silver and gold.

"Now I wonder what this can be?" Pa said, as he lifted from the very bottom of the barrel something bulky and lumpy that was wrapped around and around with thick brown paper.

"Je-ru-salem crickets!" he exclaimed. "If it isn't our Christmas turkey, still frozen solid!"

He held the great turkey up where all could see. "And fat! Fifteen pounds or I miss my guess." And as he let the mass of brown paper fall, it thumped on the floor and out of it rolled several cranberries.

"And if here isn't a package of cranberries to go with it!" said Pa.

Carrie shrieked with delight. Mary clasped her hands and said, "Oh my!" But Ma asked, "Did the groceries come for the stores, Charles?"

"Yes, sugar and flour and dried fruit and meat—oh, everything any-body needs," Pa answered.

"Well then, Mr. Boast, you bring Mrs. Boast day after tomorrow," Ma said. "Come as early as you can and we will celebrate the springtime with a Christmas dinner."

"That's the ticket!" Pa shouted, while Mr. Boast threw back his head and the room filled with his ringing laugh. They all joined in, for no one could help laughing when Mr. Boast did.

"We'll come! You bet we'll come!" Mr. Boast chortled. "Christmas dinner in May! That will be great, to feast after a winter of darn near fasting! I'll hurry home and tell Ellie."

Christmas in May

Pa bought groceries that afternoon. It was wonderful to see him coming in with armfuls of packages, wonderful to see a whole sack of white flour, sugar, dried apples, soda crackers, and cheese. The kerosene can was full. How happy Laura was to fill the lamp, polish the chimney, and trim the wick. At suppertime the light shone through the clear glass onto the red-checked tablecloth and the white biscuits, the warmed up potatoes, and the platter of fried salt pork.

With yeast cakes, Ma set the sponge for light bread that night, and she put the dried apples to soak for pies.

Laura did not need to be called next morning. She was up at dawn, and all day she helped Ma bake and stew and boil the good things for next day's Christmas dinner.

Early that morning Ma added water and flour to the bread sponge and set it to rise again. Laura and Carrie picked over the cranberries and washed them. Ma stewed them with sugar until they were a mass of crimson jelly.

Laura and Carrie carefully picked dried raisins from their long stems and carefully took the seeds out of each one. Ma stewed the dried apples, mixed the raisins with them, and made pies.

"It seems strange to have everything one could want to work with," said Ma. "Now I have cream of tartar and plenty of saleratus, I shall make a cake."

All day long the kitchen smelled of good things, and when night came the cupboard held large brown-crusted loaves of white bread, a sugar-frosted loaf of cake, three crisp-crusted pies, and the jellied cranberries.

"I wish we could eat them now," Mary said. "Seems like I can't wait till tomorrow."

"I'm waiting for the turkey first," said Laura, "and you may have sage in the stuffing, Mary."

She sounded generous but Mary laughed at her. "That's only because there aren't any onions for you to use!"

"Now, girls, don't get impatient," Ma begged them. "We will have a loaf of light bread and some of the cranberry sauce for supper."

So the Christmas feasting was begun the night before.

It seemed too bad to lose any of that happy time in sleep. Still, sleeping was the quickest way to tomorrow morning. It was no time at all, after Laura's eyes closed, till Ma was calling her and tomorrow was today.

What a hurrying there was! Breakfast was soon over, then while Laura and Carrie cleared the table and washed the dishes, Ma prepared the big turkey for roasting and mixed the bread-stuffing for it.

The May morning was warm and the wind from the prairie smelled of springtime. Doors were open and both rooms could be used once more. Going in and out of the large front room whenever she wanted to, gave Laura a spacious and rested feeling, as if she could never be cross again.

Ma had already put the rocking chairs by the front windows to get them out of her way in the kitchen. Now the turkey was in the oven, and

Mary helped Laura draw the table into the middle of the front room. Mary raised its drop-leaves and spread smoothly over it the white table-cloth that Laura brought her. Then Laura brought the dishes from the cupboard and Mary placed them around the table.

Carrie was peeling potatoes and Grace was running races with herself the length of both rooms.

Ma brought the glass bowl filled with glowing cranberry jelly. She set it in the middle of the white tablecloth and they all admired the effect.

"We do need some butter to go with the light bread, though," Ma said.

"Never mind, Caroline," said Pa. "There's tar-paper at the lumberyard now. I'll soon fix up the shanty and we'll move out to the homestead in a few days."

The roasting turkey was filling the house with scents that made their mouths water. The potatoes were boiling and Ma was putting the coffee on when Mr. and Mrs. Boast came walking in.

"For the last mile, I've been following my nose to that turkey!" Mr. Boast declared.

"I was thinking more of seeing the folks, Robert, than of anything to eat," Mrs. Boast chided him. She was thin and the lovely rosy color was gone from her cheeks, but she was the same darling Mrs. Boast, with the same laughing black-fringed blue eyes and the same dark hair curling under the same brown hood. She shook hands warmly with Ma and Mary and Laura and stooped down to draw Carrie and Grace close in her arms while she spoke to them.

"Come into the front room and take off your things, Mrs. Boast," Ma urged her. "It is good to see you again after so long. Now you rest in the rocking chair and visit with Mary while I finish up dinner."

"Let me help you," Mrs. Boast asked, but Ma said she must be tired after her long walk and everything was nearly ready.

"Laura and I will soon have dinner on the table," said Ma, turning quickly back to the kitchen. She ran against Pa in her haste.

"We better make ourselves scarce, Boast," said Pa. "Come along, and I'll show you the *Pioneer Press* I got this morning."

"It will be good to see a newspaper again," Mr. Boast agreed eagerly. So the kitchen was left to the cooks.

"Get the big platter to put the turkey on," Ma said, as she lifted the heavy dripping-pan out of the oven.

Laura turned to the cupboard and saw on the shelf a package that had not been there before.

"What's that, Ma?" she asked.

"I don't know. Look and see," Ma told her, and Laura undid the paper. There on a small plate was a ball of butter.

"Butter! It's butter!" she almost shouted.

They heard Mrs. Boast laugh. "Just a little Christmas present!" she called.

Pa and Mary and Carrie exclaimed aloud in delight and Grace squealed long and shrill while Laura carried the butter to the table. Then she hurried back to slide the big platter carefully beneath the turkey as Ma raised it from the dripping-pan.

While Ma made the gravy Laura mashed the potatoes. There was no milk, but Ma said, "Leave a very little of the boiling water in, and after you mash them beat them extra hard with the big spoon."

The potatoes turned out white and fluffy, though not with the flavor that plenty of hot milk and butter would have given them.

When all the chairs were drawn up to the well-filled table, Ma looked at Pa and every head bowed.

"Lord, we thank Thee for all Thy bounty." That was all Pa said, but it seemed to say everything.

"The table looks some different from what it did a few days ago," Pa said as he heaped Mrs. Boast's plate with turkey and stuffing and potatoes and a large spoonful of cranberries. And as he went on filling the plates he added, "It has been a long winter."

"And a hard one," said Mr. Boast.

"It is a wonder how we all kept well and came through it," Mrs. Boast said.

While Mr. and Mrs. Boast told how they had worked and contrived through that long winter, all alone in the blizzard-bound shanty on their claim, Ma poured the coffee and Pa's tea. She passed the bread and the butter and the gravy and reminded Pa to refill the plates.

When every plate had been emptied a second time Ma refilled the cups and Laura brought on the pies and the cake.

They sat a long time at the table, talking of the winter that was past and the summer to come. Ma said she could hardly wait to get back to the homestead. The wet, muddy roads were the difficulty now, but Pa and Mr. Boast agreed that they would dry out before long. The Boasts were

glad that they had wintered on their claim and didn't have to move back to it now.

At last they all left the table. Laura brought the red-bordered table cover and Carrie helped her to spread it to cover neatly out of sight the food and the empty dishes. Then they joined the others by the sunny window.

Pa stretched his arms above his head. He opened and closed his hands and stretched his fingers wide, then ran them through his hair till it all stood on end.

"I believe this warm weather has taken the stiffness out of my fingers," he said. "If you will bring me the fiddle, Laura, I'll see what I can do."

Laura brought the fiddle-box and stood close by while Pa lifted the fiddle out of its nest. He thumbed the strings and tightened the keys as he listened. Then he rosined the bow and drew it across the strings.

A few clear, true notes softly sounded. The lump in Laura's throat almost choked her.

Pa played a few bars and said, "This is a new song I learned last fall, the time we went to Volga to clear the tracks. You hum the tenor along with the fiddle, Boast, while I sing it through the first time. A few times over, and you'll all pick up the words."

They all gathered around him to listen while he played again the opening bars. Then Mr. Boast's tenor joined the fiddle's voice and Pa's voice singing:

> *"This life is a difficult riddle,*
>
> *For how many people we see*
>
> *With faces as long as a fiddle*
>
> *That ought to be shining with glee.*
>
> *I am sure in this world there are plenty*
>
> *Of good things enough for us all*
>
> *And yet there's not one out of twenty*
>
> *But thinks that his share is too small.*

> *"Then what is the use of repining,*
>
> *For where there's a will there's a way,*
>
> *And tomorrow the sun may be shining,*
>
> *Although it is cloudy today.*

"Do you think that by sitting and sighing

You'll ever obtain all you want?

It's cowards alone that are crying

And foolishly saying, 'I can't!'

It is only by plodding and striving

And laboring up the steep hill

Of life, that you'll ever be thriving

Which you'll do if you've only the will."

They were all humming the melody now and when the chorus came again, Mrs. Boast's alto, Ma's contralto, and Mary's sweet soprano joined Mr. Boast's tenor and Pa's rich bass, singing the words, and Laura sang, too, soprano:

"Then what is the use of repining,

For where there's a will, there's a way,

And tomorrow the sun may be shining,

Although it is cloudy today."

And as they sang, the fear and the suffering of the long winter seemed to rise like a dark cloud and float away on the music. Spring had come. The sun was shining warm, the winds were soft, and the green grass growing.

CHRISTMAS IN THE GOLDEN YEARS

It's Christmas Eve and a storm is coming! That means Christmas Day will be spent at home instead of at church in town, and so Laura, Carrie, and Grace scurry about in preparation for their Christmas celebration. Mary is away this year at a school for the blind, and as Laura thinks back to all the merry Christmases gone by, she wishes with all her heart that her dear sister could be there with them. And oh, how Laura misses Almanzo! When a surprise visitor knocks on the door, Laura receives the most special Christmas gift she could ever have hoped for. Merry Christmas, Laura!

The Night Before Christmas

On Christmas Eve again, there was a Christmas tree at the church in town. In good time, the Christmas box had gone to Mary, and the house was full of Christmas secrets as the girls hid from each other to wrap the presents for the Christmas tree. But at ten o'clock that morning, snow began to fall.

Still it seemed that it might be possible to go to the Christmas tree. All the afternoon Grace watched from the window, and once or twice the wind moderated. By suppertime, however, it was howling at the eaves, and the air was thick with flying snow.

"It's too dangerous to risk it," Pa said. It was a straight wind, blowing steadily, but you never could tell; it might turn into a blizzard while the people were in the church.

No plans had been made for Christmas Eve at home, so everyone had much to do. In the kitchen Laura was popping corn in the iron kettle set into a hole of the stove top from which she had removed the stove lid. She put a handful of salt into the kettle; when it was hot she put in a handful of popcorn. With a long-handled spoon she stirred it, while with the other hand she held the kettle's cover to keep the corn from flying out as it popped. When it stopped popping she dropped in another handful of corn and kept on stirring, but now she need not hold the cover, for the popped white kernels stayed on top and kept the popping kernels from jumping out of the kettle.

Ma was boiling molasses in a pan. When Laura's kettle was full of popped corn, Ma dipped some into a large pan, poured a thin trickle of the boiling molasses over it, and then buttering her hands, she deftly squeezed handfuls of it into popcorn balls. Laura kept popping corn and Ma made it into balls until the large dishpan was heaped with their sweet crispness.

In the sitting room Carrie and Grace made little bags of pink mosquito netting, left over last summer from the screen door. They filled the bags with Christmas candy that Pa had brought from town that week.

"It's lucky I thought we'd want more candy than we'd likely get at the Christmas tree," Pa took credit to himself.

"Oh!" Carrie discovered. "We've made one bag too many. Grace miscounted."

"I did not!" Grace cried.

"Grace," Ma said.

"I am not contradicting!" cried Grace.

"Grace," said Pa.

Grace gulped. "Pa," she said. "I didn't count wrong. I guess I can count five! There was candy enough for another one, and it looks pretty in the pink bag."

"So it does, and it is nice to have an extra one. We haven't always been so lucky," Pa told her.

Laura remembered the Christmas on the Verdigris River in Indian Territory, when Mr. Edwards had walked eighty miles to bring her and Mary each one stick of candy. Wherever he was tonight, she wished him as much happiness as he had brought them. She remembered the Christmas Eve on Plum Creek in Minnesota, when Pa had been lost in the blizzard and they feared he would never come back. He had eaten the Christmas candy while he lay sheltered three days under the creek bank. Now here they were, in the snug warm house, with plenty of candy and other good things.

Yet now she wished that Mary were there, and she was trying not to think of Almanzo. When he first went away, letters had come from him often; then they had come regularly. Now for three weeks there had been no letter. He was at home, Laura thought, meeting his old friends and the girls he used to know. Springtime was four months away. He might forget her, or wish that he had not given her the ring that sparkled on her finger.

Pa broke into her thoughts. "Bring me the fiddle, Laura. Let's have a little music before we begin on these good things."

She brought him the fiddle box and he tuned the fiddle and rosined the bow. "What shall I play?"

"Play Mary's song first," Laura answered. "Perhaps she is thinking of us."

Pa drew the bow across the strings and he and the fiddle sang:

"Ye banks and braes and streams around

The castle of Montgomery,

Green be your woods and fair your flowers,

Your waters never drumlie;

There summer first unfolds her robes

And there the langest tarry,

For there I took the last fareweel

Of my sweet Highland Mary."

One Scots song reminded Pa of another, and with the fiddle he sang:

"My heart is sair, I dare na tell,

My heart is sair for somebody.

Oh! I could wake a winter night,

A' for the sake o' somebody."

Ma sat in her rocking chair beside the heater, and Carrie and Grace were snug in the window seat, but Laura moved restlessly around the room.

The fiddle sang a wandering tune of its own that made her remember June's wild roses. Then it caught up another tune to blend with Pa's voice.

"When marshalled on the mighty plane,

The glittering hosts bestud the sky

One star alone of all the train

Can catch the sinner's wandering eye.

It was my light, my guide, my all,

It bade my dark forebodings cease,

And through the storm and dangers thrall

It led me to the port of peace.

Now safely moored, my perils o'er,

I'll sing, first in night's diadem

Forever and forever more,

The Star—the Star of Bethlehem."

Grace said softly, "The Christmas star."

The fiddle sang to itself again while Pa cocked his head, listening.

"The wind is rising," he said. "Good thing we stayed home."

Then the fiddle began to laugh and Pa's voice laughed as he sang,

"Oh, do not stand so long outside,

Why need you be so shy?

The people's ears are open, John,

As they are passing by!

You can not tell what they may think

They've said strange things before

And if you wish to talk awhile,

Come in and shut the door!

Come in! Come in! Come in!"

Laura looked at Pa in amazement as he sang so loudly, looking at the door, "Come in! Come in! Come . . ."

Someone knocked at the door. Pa nodded to Laura to go to the door, while he ended the song. "Come in and shut the door!"

A gust of wind swirled snow into the room when Laura opened the door; it blinded her for a moment and when she could see she could not believe her eyes. The wind whirled snow around Almanzo as, speechless, she stood holding the door open.

"Come in!" Pa called. "Come in and shut the door!" Shivering, he laid the fiddle in its box and put more coal on the fire. "That wind blows the cold into a fellow's bones," he said. "What about your team?"

"I drove Prince, and I put him in the stable beside Lady," Almanzo answered, as he shook the snow from his overcoat and hung it with his cap on the polished buffalo horns fastened to the wall near the door, while Ma rose from her chair to greet him.

Laura had retreated to the other end of the room, beside Carrie and Grace. When Almanzo looked toward them, Grace said, "I made an extra bag of candy."

"And I brought some oranges," Almanzo answered, taking a paper bag from his overcoat pocket. "I have a package with Laura's name on it, too, but isn't she going speak to me?"

"I can't believe it is you," Laura murmured. "You said you would be gone all winter."

"I decided I didn't want to stay away so long, and as you will speak to me, here is your Christmas gift."

"Come, Charles, put the fiddle away," said Ma. "Carrie and Grace, help me bring in the popcorn balls."

Laura opened the small package that Almanzo gave her. The white paper unfolded; there was a white box inside. She lifted its lid. There in a nest of soft white cotton lay a gold bar pin. On its flat surface was etched a little house, and before it along the bar lay a tiny lake, and a spray of grasses and leaves.

"Oh, it is beautiful," she breathed. "Thank you!"

"Can't you thank a fellow better than that?" he asked, and then he put his arms around her while Laura kissed him and whispered, "I am glad you came back."

Pa came from the kitchen bringing a hodful of coal and Ma followed. Carrie brought in the pan of popcorn balls and Grace gave everyone a bag of candy.

While they ate the sweets, Almanzo told of driving all day in the cold winds and camping on the open prairie with no house nor shelter near, as he and Royal drove south into Nebraska. He told of seeing the beautiful capital building at Omaha; of muddy roads when they turned east into Iowa, where the farmers were burning their corn for fuel because they could not sell it for as much as twenty-five cents a bushel. He told of seeing the Iowa state capital at Des Moines; of rivers in flood that they crossed in Iowa and Missouri, until when faced with the Missouri River they turned north again.

So with interesting talk the evening sped by until the old clock struck twelve.

"Merry Christmas!" Ma said, rising from her chair, and "Merry Christmas!" everyone answered.

Almanzo put on his overcoat, his cap and mittens, said good night, and went out into the storm. Faintly the sleigh bells rang as he passed the house on his way home.

"Did you hear them before?" Laura asked Pa.

"Yes, and nobody was ever asked to come in oftener than he was," said Pa. "I suppose he couldn't hear me in the storm."

"Come, come, girls," Ma said. "If you don't get to sleep soon, Santa

Claus will have no chance to fill the stockings."

In the morning, there would be all the surprises from the stockings, and at noon there would be the special Christmas feast, with a big fat hen stuffed and roasted, brown and juicy, and Almanzo would be there, for Ma had asked him to Christmas dinner. The wind was blowing hard, but it had not the shriek and howl of a blizzard wind, so probably he would be able to come tomorrow.

"Oh, Laura!" Carrie said, as Laura blew out the lamp in the bedroom. "Isn't this the nicest Christmas! Do Christmases get better all the time?"

"Yes," Laura said. "They do."